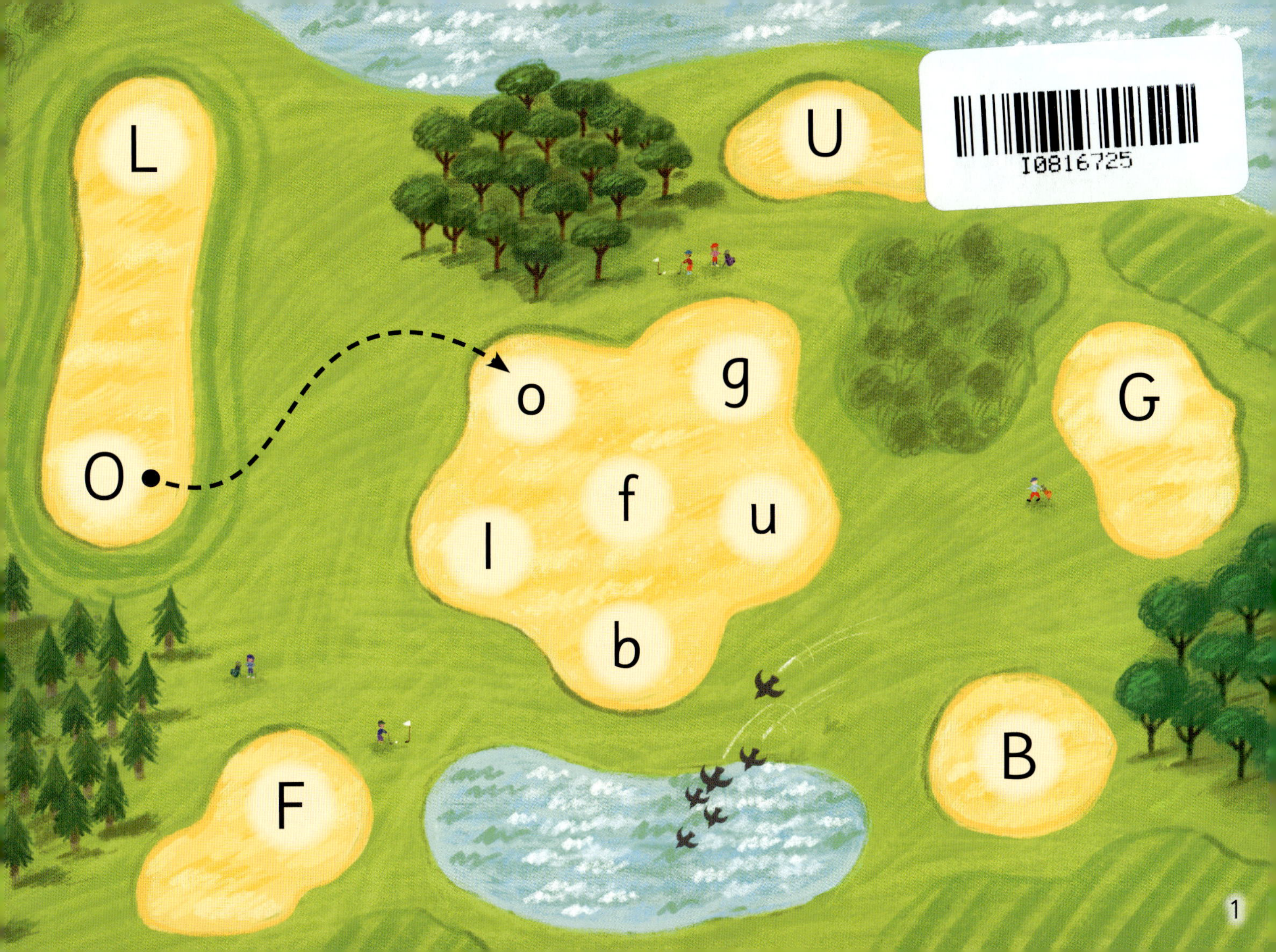
L
O
U
o
g
f
u
l
b
G
F
B
I0816725

Get up, Fred.

Fred, get up!
It’s golf at ten.

Golf?
But golf is dull.

Nonsense! It's fun.
Get dressed.

At golf...

- sun
- Dad
- cap
- golf club
- socks
- Fred
- comic strip

It's hot, Dad.
It's not.
It's splendid!

Fred is fed up.

Dad is stuck in sand.

Dad is glum and cross.
sand
mud
muck

His golf club is bent.

Golf is not fun.